Amelia Ann Blanford Edwards

Ballads

Amelia Ann Blanford Edwards

Ballads

ISBN/EAN: 9783744770736

Printed in Europe, USA, Canada, Australia, Japan

Cover: Foto ©Andreas Hilbeck / pixelio.de

More available books at **www.hansebooks.com**

BALLADS.

BY THE

AUTHOR OF "BARBARA'S HISTORY."

"BALLAD: A meaner kind of popular song."
Webster's Dictionary.

LONDON :

TINSLEY BROTHERS, 18, CATHERINE ST., STRAND.

1865.

BRADBURY AND EVANS, PRINTERS, WHITEFRIARS.

TO

MY MOST BELOVED FRIEND,

ELLEN BRAYSHER.

THE little Ballads here gathered together were nearly all written for music. Perhaps I scarcely knew till now how much of their melody they owed to the composers who set them, or how much of their meaning to the sweet voices that sang them. In their present form, however, they are too effectually disenchanted to leave me in any doubt as to the slenderness of those intrinsic merits upon which my rhymes must now stand.

AMELIA B. EDWARDS.

CONTENTS.

—◆—

x   CONTENTS.

RELIQUIÆ.

A WILD, wet night! The driving sleet

    Blurs all the lamps along the quay;

The windows shake; the busy street

Is yet alive with hurrying feet;

    The wind raves from the sea!

So let it rave! My lamp burns bright;

    My long day's work is almost done;

I curtain out each sound and sight—

Of all nights in the year, to-night

　I choose to be alone.

Alone, with doors and windows fast,

　Before my open desk I stand . . . .

Alas! can twelve long months be past,

My hidden, hidden wealth, since last

　I held thee in my hand?

So, there it lies!　From year to year

　I see the ribbon change; the page

Turn yellower; and the very tear

That blots the writing, disappear

　And fade away with age!

Mine eyes grow dim when they behold

   The precious trifles hoarded there—

A ring of batter'd Indian gold,

A wither'd harebell, and a fold

   Of sunny chesnut hair !

Not all the riches of the earth,

   Not all the treasures of the sea,

Could buy these house-gods from my hearth

And yet, the secret of their worth

   Must live and die with me.

LONELY.

Sitting lonely, ever lonely,

Waiting, waiting for one only,

Thus I mourn the weary moments passing by;

And the heavy evening gloom

Gathers slowly in the room,

And the chill November darkness dims the sky.

Now the countless busy feet

Cross each other in the street,

And I watch the faces flitting past my door;

But the step that linger'd nightly,

And the hand that rapp'd so lightly,

And the eyes that beam'd so brightly,

Come no more !

By the firelight's fitful gleaming

I am dreaming, ever dreaming,

And the rain is slowly falling all around;

And voices that are nearest,

Of friends the best and dearest,

Appear to have a strange and distant sound.

Now the weary wind is sighing,

And the murky day is dying,

And the wither'd leaves lie scatter'd round my door;

But that voice whose whisper'd greeting

Set this heart so wildly beating

At each fond and frequent meeting,

Comes no more !

SERENADE.

THE winds are all hush'd and the moon is high,

Like a queen on her silver throne.

Tranquil and dusk the woodlands lie ;

Scarcely a cloud sails over the sky ;

None are awake save the stars and I—

Sleepest thou still, mine own ?

The song of the nightingale stirs the air,

And the breath of the briar is blown.

Come forth in thy beauty beyond compare!

I'll clasp thee close, and I'll call thee fair ;

And I'll kiss off the dew from thy golden hair—

Sleepest thou still, mine own ?

DESERTED.

THE river flow'd past with the light on its breast,

And the weeds went eddying by,

And the round red sun sank down in the West

When my love's loving lips to my lips were prest,

Under the evening sky.

Now weeping alone by the river I stray,

For my love he has left me this many a day,

Left me to droop and die !

As the river flow'd then, the river flows still,

  In ripple, and foam, and spray,

On by the church, and round by the hill,

And under the sluice of the old burnt mill,

  And out to the fading day.

    But I love it no more, for delight grows cold

    When the song is sung, and the tale is told,

    And the heart is giv'n away!

Oh, river, run far! Oh, river, run fast!

  Oh, weeds, float out to the sea!

For the sun has gone down on my beautiful past,

And the hopes that like bread on the waters I cast

  Have drifted away like thee!

So the dream it is fled, and the day it is done,

And my lips still murmur the name of one

Who will never come back to me!

WILD BELLS.

I MET her in the quiet lane

One Sabbath morning early;

The sun was bright, although the rain

Still glitter'd on the barley.

The lark was singing to his mate;

The wild bells chimed their warning;

We paused awhile outside the gate—

We linger'd till it was too late

To go to church that morning!

Again we met. The whisp'ring leaves

   Danced high in light and shadow ;

The reapers piled the yellow sheaves ;

   The bees humm'd o'er the meadow.

The royal sun rose up in state,

   Our marriage-day adorning ;—

The bells rang out ; wide stood the gate ;

And neither of us was too late

   To go to church *that* morning !

THOSE OTHER TIMES.

THOSE other times! those other times!

That dream of passion past and o'er!

Can other times and other climes

Come back once more?

So sweet, so fair, so long gone by,

Remember'd only with a sigh

In my sad rhymes!

Those other times! those other times!

How strange and subtle are their spells!

Once more I hear the airy chimes

Of village bells.

Once more that voice so long unheard

Whispers my name, and blends the word

With my sad rhymes!

EURYDICE.

Must these eyes no more behold thee,

Eurydice?

Shall these arms no more enfold thee,

Eurydice?

Alas! in dreams I sometimes meet thee,

As we met ere Hades' portal

Closed between us; and I greet thee,

Call thee mine, and deem thee mortal,

Eurydice!

Call thee mine as, hand in hand,

We wander by the well-known strand,

Eurydice!

Call thee mine, and softly sing

One of the old passionate lays,

Touching here and there a string,

In the pauses of my praise—

Touching here and there a string

Of the old God-given lute,

While the charmèd sea-bird, mute,

Hovers on suspended wing!

Dreaming thus, I hear thee speak,

Eurydice!

I feel thy warm breath on my cheek,

Eurydice !

I see thine eyes reflect my own,

I kiss thy hair, I clasp thy hands,

I mark our double shadow thrown

Along the lengthening sands.

I crown thee with the wild sea-flowers,

Eurydice !

The happy days go by like hours,

Eurydice !

Then, shelter'd from the noonday heat,

In fragrant depths of mossy caves

Thou sleepest, and the little waves

Steal up and kiss thy feet.

So I woo'd thee, so I won thee,

As the evening shades were creeping

O'er the sunshine of the meadows,

Eurydice!

Canst thou hear me call upon thee,

Eurydice?

Art thou near me in my sleeping?

Stray no echoes of my weeping

To the land of shadows?

ANOTHER SERENADE.

SLEEP, dearest, sleep!

The silver moon is shining—

Over the throbbing sea,

The beating, passionate sea,

Her virgin brow inclining,

As I incline o'er thee!

Sleep! sleep!

Sleep, dearest, sleep!

The world at peace is lying—

Only the night-winds free,

The passionate night-winds free,

Around thy door are sighing,

As I sigh for thee!

Sleep! sleep!

MARGUERITE.

MOCKING little Marguerite!

Artful little Marguerite!

   See how she loves to tease me—

Just now her words were soft and sweet,

   As if she meant to please me;

Yet, look you, if we chance to meet

To-morrow in the village street,

She'll be so cruelly discreet,

    Her very looks will freeze me!

Saucy little Marguerite!

Scornful little Marguerite!

    She'll sometimes try to charm me;

Or else, her triumph to complete,

    With cold disdain alarm me.

And then, with laughter wild and sweet,

She'll taunt me with my own defeat,

Dance round me on bright twinkling feet,

    And once again disarm me!

Heartless little Marguerite!

Faithless little Marguerite!

I vow you've so bewitch'd me

That I am more than half inclined

To call your very scornings kind,

And swear that though my peace of mind

Be stolen, you've enrich'd me !

LONG AGO.

Do you remember, brother mine,

That quaint old farmhouse on the Tyne

Where you and I were born—

The gabled roofs, the gilded vanes,

The windows with their diamond panes

That glitter'd to the morn ?

And do you recollect the hill

Behind the house ?   I see it still,

All dotted o'er with sheep;

And, farther off, the solemn woods

Above whose leafy solitudes

Arose the castle keep.

We thought an ogre gaunt and grim,

Who long'd to tear us limb from limb,

Dwelt in that ruin'd tow'r;

And bitterly we used to dread

The gloomy journey up to bed,

When came th' appointed hour.

Then all the giants kill'd by Jack

Lurk'd in the hall and dragg'd us back,

Outside the parlor door—

Perchance 'twas but my skirt had caught;

But oh! my horror when I thought

'Twas clutch'd for evermore!

And then, when we had said good night,

And Janet took away the light

And left us in our beds,

Do you remember how we two

Lay dumb and trembling, as we drew

The blankets o'er our heads?

Then what dread fingers tried the doors,

What stealthy footsteps trod the floors,

What eyes glared through the gloom!

What cracks the wainscot gave! What hosts

Of Afreets, Genii, Ghouls, and Ghosts

   Did people all the room!

Such is life's fickleness! The fears

That cost our youth so many tears,

   Provoke our smiles to-day;

And tales which then were our delight

When read by day, became by night

   Our torture and dismay.

THE RHINE-MAIDEN.

'TWAS in the sunny Rhineland

As the golden day was ending ;

The ripe grapes in the vine-land

Were in purple clusters bending ;

The ruin'd tower on the height

Was glowing in the crimson light

The western sun was lending.

I saw her then—I see her yet—

It was the first time that we met

In the sunny Rhineland!

I saw her standing all alone;

The chapel bells were ringing;

And, mingled with the organ's tone,

I heard her gentle singing.

The river ran beside her feet,

And oh! her voice so clear and sweet

Seem'd like the lark's upspringing!

I saw her thus at close of day;

I gazed—and gazed my heart away,

In the sunny Rhineland!

Upon her image in the stream,

  All broken 'midst the rushes,

She gazes in a happy dream,

  And smiles, and sighs, and blushes.

She takes the arrow from her hair,

And down upon her shoulders fair

  The golden shower gushes!

    I watch'd her as I stood apart—

    That silver arrow pierced my heart,

    In the sunny Rhineland!

WINTER SONG.

THE wintry wind sweeps down the plain,

The larches bend like rushes,

The frost makes pictures on the pane,

The torrent wears an icy chain,

The babbling streamlet hushes.

The silent lake is frozen o'er,

One solid flat from shore to shore,

Where every sledge its progress tells

With merriment of silver bells !

The Boreal lights at midnight show,

   The stars above us shiver ;

At morn, when to the chase we go,

We see the wolf-track in the snow

   By windings of the river.

And then, towards declining day,

We hasten on our homeward way

To where yon window warms the night

With glowings of a ruddy light !

TO ———.

Ah, faithless! all this winter long

   My pain has been thy pastime!

I loved with heart, and soul, and song—

Thine all the sport; mine all the wrong . .

   Beware! it is the last time.

What though my love at times were shown

   In somewhat silent fashion,

Thou read'st it plainly—thou alone—

In ev'ry glance, and ev'ry tone

· That told the tale of passion !

'Tis now thy turn to plead in vain,

  And my turn to deny thee.

I know thee, lady—thou would'st fain

Thyself undo the darling chain :—

  Thou canst not. I defy thee.

Thou know'st not what an iron will

  Despair like mine can borrow ;

For, be it well, or be it ill,

I feel that I must hold thee still, ·

  In sin, or shame, or sorrow !

Yes, mine thou art and still shalt be,

Despite thine own endeavour ;

Nor life, nor death shall set thee free,

And neither heav'n, nor earth, nor sea,

Thy lot from mine shall sever !

MANY A TIME AND OFT.

WHEN the house is still, and the day is done,

   And the stars are out aloft,

I sit by the failing fire alone,

And think of the years that are past and gone,

   Many a time and oft.

     I dream of that village beside the sea;

     I dream of that seat by the trysting-tree;

     And of one who will never come back to me—

     Ah! many a time and oft!

When the city is hush'd, and the chimes are still,

And the voice of the crowd is soft,

My thoughts wander on at their own wild will,

And my tears fall fast, and my heart is chill,

Many a time and oft.

I dream of the hopes all faded and fled,

Of the vow that is broken, the shaft that is sped,

And of one to whom I for ever am dead—

Ah! many a time and oft!

TO ZULEIKA.

THOU'RT slender as the clove,

An unblown rose in May!

'Tis long since I have dared to love,

Though silent till to-day.

Thy heart is cold as snow;

Thou smilest when I sigh—

If thou canst pity, pity now,

And speak before I die!

I gaze upon thine eyes

Through all the livelong day,

And pour my passion forth in sighs,

And look my life away.

The stars are not more bright ;

The ruby lacks their glow ;

They're deeper than the deepest night,

And darker than the sloe !

Could I for one day be

The Sultan on his throne,

And thou a maid of low degree,

Unfriended and alone,

I'd mount my milk-white barb,

   And call my guards and band,

And robe me in my richest garb

   To ask thee for thy hand.

And coming thus in state

   All through the narrow street,

I would alight before thy gate

   And kneel down at thy feet ;

And swear by heav'n and earth

   And Allah throned above,

That crown and pomp were nothing worth

   To me without thy love !

TO HASSAN.

THE tract of the desert lies weary and bare,

The chime of the camel-bell dies on the air

With the chant of the drover.

The print of thy tent, and the desolate stain

Of thy fire, my Hassan, are all that remain

Of the dream that is over!

Ah, why wert thou tempted the desert to roam ?

Of the palms and the meadows, of love and of home

Wert thou weary, my rover?

Was my sunshine of youth too unclouded to last ?

Oh, the dear yesterdays faded and past,—

Are they all over?

TORRENT SONG.

HARK! the ripple of the fountain

Dancing downward in its glee,

From its cradle in the mountain

To its grave in yonder sea.

Now 'tis sparkling through the meadow;

Now 'tis darkling through the shadow;

And the golden sun is glowing

On the streamlet in its flowing,

And it murmurs while 'tis going

" Come with me ! "

Ever swifter to the ocean

Leap the waters bright and free,

And the music of their motion

Charms the wild bird and the bee.

Now they're flying down the hill-side ;

Now they're sighing in the mill-tide ;

And the moonbeams soft and fleeting,

With the silver starlight meeting,

Kiss the waves which are repeating

" Come with me ! "

A LEGEND OF BOISGUILBERT.

BESIDE this tarn, in ages gone,

As antique legends darkly tell,

A false, false Abbot and forty monks

Did once in sinful plenty dwell.

Accursed of Christ and all the saints,

They robb'd the rich; they robb'd the poor;

They quaff'd the best of Malvoisie;

They turn'd the hungry from their door.

And though the nations groan'd aloud,

And famine stalk'd across the land—

And though the noblest Christian blood

Redden'd the thirsty Eastern sand—

These monks kept up their ancient state,

Nor cared how long the troubles lasted;

But fed their deer, and stock'd their pond,

And feasted when they should have fasted.

And so it fell one Christmas Eve,

When it was dark, and cold, and late,

A pious knight from Palestine

Came knocking at the convent gate.

He rode a steed of Arab blood ;

His helm was up ; his mien was bold ;

And round about his neck he wore

A chain of Saracenic gold.

" What ho ! good monks of Boisguilbert,

Your guest am I to-night !" quoth he.

" Have you a stable for my steed ?

A supper, and a cell for me ? "

The Abbot laugh'd ; the friars scoff'd ;

They fell upon that knight renown'd,

And bore him down, and tied his hands,

And threw him captive on the ground.

"Sir guest!" they cried, "your steed shall be

Into our convent stable led;

And, since we have no cell to spare,

Yourself must sleep among the dead!"

He mark'd them with a steadfast eye;

He heard them with a dauntless face;

He was too brave to fear to die;

He was too proud to sue for grace.

They tore the chain from round his neck,

The trophy of a gallant fight,

Whilst o'er the black and silent tarn

Their torches flash'd a sullen light.

E

And the great pike that dwelt therein,

All startled by the sudden glare,

Dived down among the water-weeds,

And darted blindly here and there.

And one white owl that made her nest

Up in the belfry tow'r hard by,

Flew round and round on swirling wings

And vanish'd with a ghostly cry.

The Abbot stood upon the brink;

He laugh'd aloud in wicked glee;

He waved his torch:—"Quick! fling him in—

Our fish shall feast to-night!" said he.

They flung him in. "Farewell!" they cried,

    And crowded round the reedy shore.

He gasping rose—"Till Christmas next!"

    He said—then sank to rise no more.

"Till Christmas next!" They stood and stared

    Into each other's guilty eyes ;   .

Then fled within the convent gates,

    Lest they should see their victim rise.

The fragile bubbles rose and broke ;

    The wid'ning circles died away ;

The white owl shriek'd again ; the pike

    Were left to silence and their prey.

A year went by.   The stealthy fogs

   Crept up the hill, all dense and slow,

And all the woods of Boisguilbert

   Lay hush'd and heavy in the snow.

The sullen sun was red by day;

   The nights were black; the winds were keen;

And all across the frozen tarn

   The footprints of the wolf were seen.

And vague foreshadowings of woe

   Beset the monks with mortal fear—

Strange shadows through the cloister pac'd—

   Strange whispers threaten'd every ear—

Strange writings started forth at dusk

   In fiery lines along the walls;

Strange spectres round the chapel sat,

   At midnight, in the sculptur'd stalls.

"Oh, father Abbot!" cried the monks,

   "We must repent! Our sins are great!

To-morrow will be Christmas Eve—

   To-morrow night may be too late!

" And should the drownèd dead arise " . . . .

The Abbot laugh'd with might and main.

" The ice," said he, " is three feet deep.

He'd find it hard to rise again !

" But when to-morrow night is come,

We'll say a mass to rest his soul ! "

To-morrow came, and all day long

The chapel bell was heard to toll.

At eve they met to read the mass.

Bent low was ev'ry shaven crown ;

One trembling monk the tapers lit ;

One held his missal upside down ;

And when their quav'ring voices in

The *Dies Iræ* all united,

Even the Abbot told his beads

And fragments of the Creed recited.

And when .... but hark ! what sounds are those ?

Is it the splitting of the ice ?

Is it a steel-clad hand that smites

Against the outer portal thrice ?

Is that the tread of an armèd heel ?

The frighten'd monks forget to pray ;

The Abbot drops the holy book ;

The *Dies Iræ* dies away ;

And in the shadow of the door

    They see their year-gone victim stand!

His rusty mail drips on the floor;

    He beckons with uplifted hand!

The Abbot rose. He could not choose;

    He had no voice or strength to pray;

For when the mighty dead command,

    The living must perforce obey.

The spectre-knight then gazed around

    With stony eye, and hand uprear'd.

" Farewell," said he, " till Christmas next!"—

    Then knight and Abbot disappear'd.

*   *   *   *   *

*   *   *   *   *

And thus it is the place is cursed,

   And long since fallen to decay;

For ev'ry Christmas Eve the knight

   Came back, and took a monk away.

Came back, while yet a blood-stain'd wretch

   The holy convent-garb profaned;

Came back while yet a guilty soul

   Of all those forty monks remain'd;

And still comes back to earth,—if we

The peasants' story may believe—

And rises from the murky tarn

At midnight every Christmas Eve !

OLD MEMORIES.

—•—

OLD memories! what spells are they

  Of sadness and delight!

They colour all my thoughts by day;

  They thread my dreams by night.

And though my hair is changing fast,

  And my eyes are almost blind,

I'm never old in that sweet past

  That lies so far behind.

Old memories! in the twilight gloom

Like phantoms they arise!

Old voices whisper through the room;

Old faces mock my eyes;

Old footsteps linger round my door;

And oh! 'mid dreams like these

My faded roses bloom once more . . . .

Keep green, old memories!

FOR EVER.

I'VE loved thee long; I love thee now;

And years have thus gone by.

A cold and careless mistress thou—

A silent suitor I.

Silent no more! The time has come

When I can be no longer dumb;

When I must speak, or die.

The fondest and the truest heart

    I've given thee, and never

Have dared to ask thee if thou art

    Indiff'rent to the giver.

        Nay, take it, break it, 'tis thine own,

        As I am thine, and thine alone

        For ever, and for ever!

Yet let thine own sweet lips express

    My fate and thy decree.

I must have either more or less,

    Wear fetters, or be free!

        Speak, for my peace hangs on thy breath,

        And be it life, or be it death,

        I'll either take from thee.

THE STUDENT.

Oh, lady, thou art fair and free

   As are the heav'ns above thee !

A student I, of low degree,

From lands that lie beyond the sea,

   Who yet hath dared to love thee !

Thou hast been taught that rank and state

   Are gifts beyond all prizing.

The poet singing at thy gate

Were all too lowly for thy hate,

Too poor for thy despising.

So proud art thou! so angel sweet!

In silence I adore thee!

And oh! whene'er we chance to meet,

I stand back in the public street,

And bare my head before thee.

'Tis said thou soon wilt wedded be

To one of princely birth—

I would the bells that peal for thee

Might toll the morrow morn for me,

And I be laid in earth.

What gallant party passes by

With plumes and pennons flying—

Thy wedding train ? Nay, then, will I

Straight in thy path all prostrate lie . . . .

One look, love !—I am dying !

RETROSPECTIVE.

Do you mind the auld past years

When we were young together ?

When the present had no tears,

And the future had no fears,

And we pluck'd the purple heather,

Frae the mountain side ?

Ah ! you were but a callant, Ben,

And I was just a lassie then,

And thought to be your bride !

Your step, Ben, was mair light,

And my cheek, I know, was fairer ;

And the stars they shone mair bright

When the gloaming turn'd to night ;

And the early flowers were rarer

On the mountain side !

Ah ! you were but a callant, Ben,

And I was just a lassie then,

And thought to be your bride !

JOAN OF ARC.

THE hostile flag from yonder height

   Waves haughtily on high :

Oh, Frenchmen, shall that hateful sight

Another day—another night—

   Our royal liege defy ?

Shall strangers offer before our shrines ?

Shall strangers gather our golden vines ?

   Or shall the foemen die ?

Charger and steed and helm prepare,

For Frenchmen do when Frenchmen dare,

Beneath their native sky.

Up, knights of Anjou and Touraine !

Up, gallant hearts of Aquitaine !

The king shall be king over France again !

What Frenchman, vassal, serf, or knight,

For freedom will not die ?

At Taillebourg, in the famous fight

'Twixt British might and Gallic right,

Did Louis' legions fly ?

Six feet of earth on the battle plain,

Six feet of earth to each foeman slain,

King Charles will not deny !

Banquet, and wreath, and bower prepare,

Maidens ! your lovers will soon be there,

After the victory !

Up, knights of Anjou and Touraine !

Up, gallant hearts of Aquitaine !

The king shall be king over France again !

PARTING.

'TWAS by the rustling sallow
  That droops above the pond;
The plough stood in the fallow,
  On the dusky slope beyond.

We linger'd near the farmhouse door,
  With fingers fast entwined,
While the sinking sun went down before
  And the moon rose up behind.

We stood there in the quiet hour ;

We could not say " farewell."

Our tears dropp'd down on grass and flower,

And glisten'd where they fell.

Our bitter tears fell fast; we sigh'd ;

But ne'er a word we said.

I wonder if the daisies died

On which that dew was shed ?

We parted as the crimson light

Just faded from the west,

When half the sky with stars was bright,

And all the world at rest.

We parted—parted—nevermore

   In fair or stormy weather

To meet again by sea or shore,

   Or see the sun together.

And if I knew that sun would rise

   No more upon my sight,

How gladly would I close my eyes

   And say my prayers to-night!

IMPORTUNITY.

I'VE waited long enough, Kathleen,

The winter's fairly past ;

The lambs are playing on the green ;

The swallow's come at last.

The vine is leafy round my door ;

The blossom's on the May ;

The waves come dancing to the shore—

Why don't you name the day ?

You know you put me off, Kathleen,

Until the early spring.

The skies are tranquil and serene;

The bees are on the wing;

The fisher spreads his little sail;

The mower's in the hay;

The primrose blossoms in the vale—

Why don't you name the day?

The thrush is building in the thorn,

Among the whisp'ring leaves;

The lark is busy in the corn,

The martin 'neath the eaves.

The little birds don't build in vain;

Their mates don't say them nay—

Beware!   I may not ask again

Why don't you name the day?

TO A YOUNG BRIDE,

—◆—

As painters in the childlike days of art

    Oft dipt the brush in gold, and crown'd the saint,

    And pattern'd robe and helm in fashion quaint,

Dwelling with patient love on ev'ry part :

And as the weaver in that time of old

    Weaving rich arras for Imperial gifts,

    Adept in all the artificer's shifts,

Mingled his silken threads with threads of gold :

And as the monk, transcribing psalm and pray'r,

Gospel and legend, in that pious age,

With gold and colours did adorn his page,

Making his costly labour still more rare :

So I, fair Bride, would have the golden thread

Of thy young life thus with my story wrought,

That o'er the scenes and people of my thought

A newer, richer brightness may be shed :—

So would I blazon here (for mine own fame)

The gracious consecration of thy name.

Oct. 13, 1864.

THE LEGEND OF THE BELL.[1]

LONG ago thro' Norseland roaming,

    Heard I once a Swedish rhyme;

Heard it, sitting in the gloaming

    Underneath a shady lime,

Where the village elders met

To gossip when the sun had set.

Quaintly sung, and quaintly worded,

    Half a truth and half a myth,

Thus it ran, and thus I heard it

Chanted by the dusky smith.

The dusky smith, all smoked and tann'd,

Grasping his hammer in his hand.

Anders Dag, a hardy peasant

Born on Dalecarlian soil,

When the spring was fair and pleasant

Went to shoot the capercoil—

Went, all fearless, to explore

Forests scarcely track'd before.

Onward through the pines and larches

Rooted in ancestral shade,

In and out the gothic arches

   Which the branching elm-trees made,

Anders Dag went bold and free;

But only one wild bird found he.

Late and long thro' glades and hollows

   Flutters far the wary game;

Late and long the sportsman follows,

   Swift of foot and prompt of aim.

Flits the bird upon the wing;

Flies the arrow from the string.

Flies and misses, swerves and glistens

   In the light of parting day!

Hark ! the baffled marksman listens

Breathless, and forgets his prey.

For yonder, in the tangled dell,

He hears the tinkling of a bell !

Tinkling faintly, dying slowly

On the breathless evening air ;

Rung, perchance, by hermit holy,

Kneeling at his vesper pray'r !

" Now, Mary mother, shield me well,"

Saith Anders Dag, " I'll find the bell ! "

Plunging in the thicket straightway,

On he went, and sign'd the cross,

Finding soon a ruin'd gateway

And a chapel green with moss.

So green, so lone, so overgrown

That it seem'd scarcely built of stone.

Nature, labouring to cancel

All the finger-prints of art,

Had planted saplings in the chancel,

Torn the sculptur'd screen apart,

Rent the fretted roof away,

And left all open to the day.

In the aisles the grass was growing;

Birds were building in the walls;

And the wild white bine was blowing

In the woodwork of the stalls.

And lo! where once the anthems rang,

Only the little thrushes sang!

Only the thrushes. Not a token,

Howsoever slight, to tell

That the silence had been broken

By the clamour of a bell!

Still, o'er every inch of ground

The sportsman sought, but nothing found.

Till at length, beneath the blinding

Veil of ivy everywhere,

Traced he something like the winding

    Fragment of a broken stair—

Something like a shatter'd tower,

Shrouded in a leafy bower.

Then, the knotted branches rending

    Limb from limb, and spray from spray,

Slowly, step by step ascending,

    Up that tow'r he forced his way.

Forced his way, and found the bell,

And found his arrow there as well!

There his arrow lay, half buried

    In the dust of ages gone,

And the sunset through the serried

Ivy foliage faintly shone ;

Beam and rafter half revealing,

All the rest in gloom concealing.

Last year's drifted leaves were lying

Rotting on the dusty floor,

And the startled bats were flying

Round and round, and o'er and o'er;

Whilst overhead, with silent tongue

The bell in shroud of cobwebs hung.

There it hung, a little higher

Than the level of the light,

Silent, like a hooded friar

At a penitential rite ;

Pulseless as the heart at rest

In a dead man's quiet breast.

Wakeful once at eve and matin,

Still it bore an ancient rhyme

Scroll'd in mediæval Latin,

Latin of the monkish time :—

" DEFUNCTUS PLORO : CONGREGO CLERUM :

PESTEM FUGO : LAUDO DEUM VERUM."

Lines which in a free translation

Mean—" *We weep for those who die :*

Call to prayers the congregation :

Plague and pestilence defy ;

And (so runs the pious phrase)

We the only true God praise."

Such its warning to the people

When in olden days it rung,

That lone prophet of the steeple,

Praise and pity on its tongue.

Now, alas! its work was done,

And its hearers' race was run.

Where of old a wealthy village

Warm with life and labour stood,

Where the earth to skilful tillage

  Yielded ample store of food,

Now, alas! on every side

Spread the forest dense and wide.

All the young and happy hearted,

  Just and loving, true and brave,

Wise and pious, had departed

  To that home beyond the grave

Where no sins or sorrows dwell—

" DEFUNCTUS PLORO," saith the bell.

Like a flash of intuition,

  Anders Dag all suddenly

Call'd to mind an old tradition,

   Heard in earliest infancy,

When the fireside tale went round,

And the snow lay on the ground.

How some Eastern ship, deserted

   By her crew in time of yore,

From her course by storms diverted,

   Drifted to the Swedish shore :

Rich her freight in silk and spice,

And tapestries of rare device.

Never yet did fierce invader

   Bring such woe upon the land

As that oriental trader

   Wreck'd upon the Swedish strand ;

For upon that fatal bark

   Plague and Death had set their mark.

Soon the dreaded poison flying,

   All unseen, from town to town,

Fill'd the land with dead and dying,

   Struck both prince and peasant down,

Swept whole villages away,

And slew its thousands night and day.

Rusted then in fort and furrow

   Gun and plough for service meet ;

Silent then the busy borough;

Green with grass the public street;

Closed the mart; unmann'd the walls;

And empty all the convent halls.

Even here, so ran the story,

Where the giants of the wood

Interlaced their branches hoary,

Once a happy hamlet stood,

Circled round with fence and field,

Buttress'd wall, and planted weald.

But the Plague one fatal morning

Like an armèd foe came down;

Came without one sign of warning;

Set his death-mark on the town;

Poison'd all the summer air,

And fill'd each household with despair.

Soon, alas! to every dwelling

Had the black infection spread;

Soon the chapel-bell was knelling,

Knelling hourly for the dead.

Till the place was all bereft,

And no living soul was left.

Anders Dag, flush'd with compassion,

Thinking all this legend o'er,

Smote the bell in angry fashion,

Crying—"Silence, evermore !

False thy tongue, and vain thy spell !"

"PESTEM FUGO !" said the bell.

"Yet," thought he, "it is not given

Unto simple men like me,

All the wondrous ways of Heaven

With our earthly eyes to see !

What God willeth must be well."

"LAUDO DEUM !" said the bell.

"Thro' the forest dark and lonely

Not by chance my feet were led—

Not by chance these ruins only

   Keep strange record of the dead !

God's great purpose who shall tell ?"

" LAUDO DEUM !" said the bell.

TRANSLATIONS.

H

THE LEAF AND THE BREEZE.[2]

FROM THE FRENCH OF ARNAULT.

———◆———

PARTED from thy native bough,

Whither, whither goest thou,

Leaflet frail !

From the oak tree where I grew

In the vale ;

From the woods all wet with dew

Lo ! the wind hath torn me !

Over hill and plain he flew,

And hither he hath borne me.

With him wandering for aye,

Until he forsakes me,

I with many others stray,

Heedless where he takes me :—

Where the leaf of laurel goes,

And the leaflet of the rose.

FLOWER AND BUD.

ALTERED FROM THE FRENCH.

———◆———

As I wander'd through the meadow,

Half in light and half in shadow,

All among the feeding kine,

I beheld at evening hour

A trembling flow'r, a drooping flow'r,

A faded flow'r of Eglantine.

Near it danced a blossom fair,

Just open'd to the evening air,

All diamonded with dew.

'Tis thus, thought I, we pass away,

And in our children, day by day,

Our faded youth renew.

CRUEL SPRINGTIME.

ADAPTED FROM BERANGER.

———◆———

FROM my window every morning

I have seen her at her own ;

I watch'd her all the winter through,

And (each to each unknown)

We learn'd to love in silence

With a love beyond compare,

And our kisses, interchanging,

Cross'd each other in the air.

The lindens planted all between

    Were leafless, every tree,

And we saw through their bare branches,

    All that either cared to see ;

But now the foliage intervenes

    To hide that window dear—

Ah, cruel, cruel Springtime !

    Wilt thou come with ev'ry year ?

Immur'd behind the leafy screen

    That shadows all my door,

I sit and sigh, because I see

    That angel face no more ;

That angel whom I first beheld,

    All radiant as the May,

Casting bread-crumbs to the sparrows

One bleak and snowy day.

She fed them, and they sang for joy

All down the wintry grove ;

And the season for their mating gave

The signal for our love.

Ah, lovely snow ! the summer sun

Brings nothing half so dear—

Thou cruel, cruel Springtime !

Must thou come with ev'ry year ?

Ah, cruel Springtime ! but for thee

Yon branches would disclose

My darling's face each happy morn

She rises from repose,

More blooming than the poets paint

Aurora on her way

Across the golden skies, to draw

The curtains of the day.

And but for thee my loving eyes

Might still be daily blest;

And still each evening I might say

"My star is gone to rest.

Her lamp expires—perchance she sleeps!"

Ah, wherefore art thou here,

Thou cruel, cruel Springtime!

Must thou come with ev'ry year?

I pray the winter soon may come,

The summer soon be o'er;

I long to see the fallen snow ;

I long to hear once more

The merry bounding of the hail,

And the music of the rain

As it glides in rapid streamlets

O'er the smooth sonorous pane !

Thine ancient empire, cruel Spring,

From me shall win no praise ;

What care I for thy zephyrs bland,

Thy long and garish days ?

Thy blossoms are not worth the smiles

I miss when thou art here—

Ah, cruel, cruel Springtime !

Must thou come with ev'ry year ?

NOTES.

THE LEGEND OF THE BELL.

THIS ballad is founded on the following extract from Fryxell's " History of Sweden " (translated by Mrs. Howitt), vol. i., p. 259 :—

" At this period a terrible pestilence had commenced to spread itself over the known world. In Sweden it was called the Diger Death, that is, the Great Death. It came from India, and in 1348 made such ravages in the South of Europe, that barely a third of the population survived. A continual south wind brought thick and damp vapours with it ; the air was never cleared by storms and rain, and oft-repeated earthquakes and signs in the air boded a great convulsion in nature. This plague attacked man and beast alike, but the young died most. In 1349 a ship, on board of which no living creature was found, was driven towards Bergen on the coast of Norway. The citizens thoughtlessly unloaded the vessel, which, being infected by the plague, spread the malady with alarming rapidity, which ravaged both Sweden and Norway during the year 1350. No family and no rank escaped ; whole parishes perished. In West Gothland four hundred and sixty-six priests died, and the King's two half-brothers fell victims to it. In the mining districts of Wermland one man and two girls alone survived, and many and many a mile divided the nearest neighbours. After this devastation wide tracts of land fell to the crown for want of heirs, and other districts became a wilderness which the wood soon covered ; so that even yet, in the centre of deep forests, remains of houses and fields which have been forgotten from that time are occasionally discovered. It once happened, long after the Diger Death, that a peasant in Eksparish went out one morning in spring to shoot the capercoil in a thick wood. As he missed the bird, he went to seek his arrow, which had fallen, as he thought, on a high moss-covered rock ; but when the peasant reached the place, he found it was a church, which had remained forgotten and forsaken, and was buried in trees."

This plague was known through Europe as the Black Death.

NOTE 2.

THE LEAF AND THE BREEZE.

THIS graceful little fable, of which a metrical translation is attempted in the foregoing pages, has been already done into English by Lord Macaulay, and into Italian by Giacomo Leopardi. We append the French original and the two versions above-named.

A. V. ARNAULT.

FABLE 16, LIVRE V.

— De ta tige détachée,
Pauvre feuille desséchée,
Où vas-tu ? — Je n'en sais rien.
L'orage a frappé le chêne
Qui seul était mon soutien.
De son inconstante haleine,
Le zéphyr ou l'aquilon
Depuis ce jour me promène

De la forêt à la plaine,

De la montagne au vallon.

Je vais où le vent me mène,

Sans me plaindre ou m'effrayer ;

Je vais où va toute chose,

Où va la feuille de rose

Et la feuille de laurier.

IMITAZIONE

DA GIACOMO LEOPARDI.

— Lungi dal proprio ramo,

Povera foglia frale,

Dove vai tu ? — Dal faggio

Là dov' io nacqui mi divise il vento.

Esso, tornando, a volo

Dal bosco alla campagna,

Dalla valle mi porta alla montagna.

Seco perpetuamente

Vo pellegrina, e tutto l' altro ignoro ;

Vo dove ogni altra cosa ;

Dove naturalmente,

Va la foglia di rosa,

E la foglia d' alloro.

TRANSLATION

BY LORD MACAULAY.

Thou poor leaf, so sear and frail,
Sport of every wanton gale,
Whence, and whither, dost thou fly,
Through this bleak autumnal sky ?
On a noble oak I grew,
Green, and broad, and fair to view ;
But the monarch of the shade
By the tempest low was laid.
From that time, I wander o'er
Wood and valley, hill and moor,
Wheresoe'er the wind is blowing,
Nothing caring, nothing knowing :
Thither go I, whither goes
Glory's laurel, Beauty's rose.

BRADBURY AND EVANS, PRINTERS, WHITEFRIARS.

www.ingramcontent.com/pod-product-compliance
Lightning Source LLC
Chambersburg PA
CBHW022138020726
47496CB00008B/2447